IF ONLY I COULD BE A
CLOWN

Xulon Press Elite
555 Winderley Pl, Suite 225
Maitland, FL 32751
407.339.4217
www.xulonpress.com

© 2024 by Barbara Allen Greer

Illustrated by Kelly Goss Atkinson

All rights reserved solely by the author. The author guarantees all contents are original and do not infringe upon the legal rights of any other person or work. No part of this book may be reproduced in any form without the permission of the author.

Due to the changing nature of the Internet, if there are any web addresses, links, or URLs included in this manuscript, these may have been altered and may no longer be accessible. The views and opinions shared in this book belong solely to the author and do not necessarily reflect those of the publisher. The publisher therefore disclaims responsibility for the views or opinions expressed within the work.

Paperback ISBN-13: 979-8-86850-410-5
Hardcover ISBN-13: 979-8-86850-411-2
eBook ISBN-13: 979-8-86850-412-9

When I grow up,
I think I will be a clown.

I will join the circus and go from town to town.

I will wear a big flower
that will squirt water all over
the place.

I will wear big floppy shoes
and sometimes fall flat on my face,

I will have a big, big nose,
and sometimes when I sneeze

The sneeze will be so big –
AAH CHOO!
I will fall to my knees.

There will always be smiles
and never any frowns.

This is the way it is,
if you keep company with clowns.

Yes, a clown is what
I think I will be.
I don't know why I have to wait,

because I am already three.

End

Milton Keynes UK
Ingram Content Group UK Ltd.
UKHW050626221024
450028UK00017B/159